Diana Kimpton lives in a cottage near the sea with her husband, three children, a gerbil and rather more spiders and woodlice than she would like. She gave up teaching maths to be a full-time mother and foster mother and started writing when her children no longer needed all her attention. She loves doing it – it's much better than washing dishes.

Two of her children have cystic fibrosis so she has spent many hours sitting in children's wards and has developed a long-standing interest in the needs of children in hospital. The idea for this book was born during a particularly long and boring admission and the development of it has helped to liven up several more.

I would like to thank the many people who have helped in the preparation of this book, especially the staff of Southampton General Hospital and St Mary's Hospital, Newport, Isle of Wight, whose help, advice and encouragement have been invaluable.

The
HOSPITAL
Highway Code

by Diana Kimpton

With illustrations by

Peter Kavanagh

A Piccolo Original

MACMILLAN

CHILDREN'S BOOKS

First published 1994 by Macmillan Children's Books

a division of Macmillan Publishers Limited
Cavaye Place London SW10 9PG
and Basingstoke

Associated companies throughout the world

ISBN 0–330–32957–X

3 5 7 9 8 6 4 2

A CIP catalogue record for this book is available from
the British Library

Typeset by Intype, London
Printed and bound in Great Britain by
Cox & Wyman Ltd, Reading, Berkshire

For Carol

Contents

Introduction

Have you ever noticed that films are much more frightening if you can't see the villain? It only takes a few mysterious noises and a shadow against the curtains to make you imagine a monster a thousand times worse than any special effects' department could produce.

Going to hospital is like that too. The less you know about what's happening, the scarier the ideas your imagination will produce. It's only natural to feel nervous sometimes, especially if you've never been away from home before, but the best ways to fight fear are with knowledge and a good laugh.

This book will give you both but it's only a starting point. Feel free to ask the doctors and nurses as many questions as you want. It's your body. You've every right to know what's happening to it.

First Things First

Some hospital admissions happen without warning. After all, no one plans to fall out of a tree or get run over by a bus. But if you are going in for tests or an operation, you'll have time to get ready.

If you have the chance, it's a good idea to visit the ward in advance. You'll feel more confident once you've seen where you will be staying and met some of the staff. If no one suggests a visit, why not phone and ask if you can go – they'll almost certainly agree.

PACKING

The hospital will probably send you a list of things to take with you. If not, here's one which should help.

- **Nightclothes** A dressing gown's not essential but you can take one if you want.

- **Slippers** If you don't have any, it's useful to take some sandals, plimsolls or other shoes which are easy to slip on and off.

- **Dayclothes** You'll get dressed in the daytime just as you would at home. It's always hot in hospital so choose light clothes.

- **Underwear** A couple of clean pairs of pants should be enough. If you stay long enough to need more, your mum and dad can bring some in when they visit. It will make them feel useful!

- **Towel**

- **Face flannel**

- **Comb, toothbrush, soap,** etc.

- **Any medicines you are taking at home**

- **Any equipment you need to overcome a disability** – for example, reading glasses, a hearing aid or specially adapted cutlery

If your mum or dad is staying in with you, they will need their clothes and washing things too. The hospital may also like them to bring some sheets – they can phone the ward to find out.

FOOD

Hospital food is not too bad but it won't be the same as the food you eat at home. Don't forget to tell the nurses if you are vegetarian or have other restrictions on your diet (perhaps because of your religion). No one will laugh at you and the kitchen staff will do their best to provide suitable meals.

There is usually a choice of food but it is limited. If your favourite drink, spread or cereal is not supplied, you can take some with you or ask your parents to fetch some later. Check with your nurse before you eat it, just in case it will upset your treatment. You will probably need to store it in the ward kitchen to keep it out of the reach of little hands – make sure you write your name on it or you'll lose it!

Many hospitals don't mind if you supplement their meals with food from home or local takeaways. However, some wards are less enthusiastic about the idea so check with the nurses before you get Mum to send out for a pizza . . .

THINGS TO DO

Patients aren't called patients for nothing. If you are going to be one, you'll need all the patience you can find. Being in hospital means waiting – waiting for tests, waiting to see the doctor and waiting to get better.

Although there will be things to do on the ward, it's a good idea to take some of your own as well. Of course, this book is the perfect solution but here's some other ideas too. They may also help your friends and relatives to think of presents for you.

- Drawing paper, plus pencils or felt tips

- Writing paper, envelopes and stamps

- Books to read

- Puzzle books plus pencils and eraser

- Schoolwork! – If it's term time and you are going to be in hospital for quite a long time, a teacher will probably help you keep your work up to date. It may even be possible for you to take your exams while you are there.

- Jigsaws – If they are smaller than 70cm by 36cm, they should fit on your bed table. The play worker may be able to lend you a board for larger ones.

- Playing cards and a book of patience games

- Plastic or paper model kits, knitting or sewing

- Videos (if the ward has a video player) Remember there are other children around so this isn't the place for *Nightmare on Elm Street* even if you are allowed to watch it at home.

- Personal stereo plus tapes

- Battery operated electronic games

- A cuddly toy – It may be well-worn, well-loved and accustomed to sharing your bed but it's not babyish. It's a mascot.

- Coins for the payphone

Remember to put your name on your things and not to leave valuable items lying around where they might be stolen. If you are going to be in hospital for a long time and want to take your own hair dryer, TV or stereo, it will need to be checked by the hospital electricians before you can use it.

Use this space here to make a list of anything else you need to remember to take with you.

VISITORS

Visitors are important. They provide company and a link with the outside world. By tradition, they also bring you grapes and eat them for you.

I'm sure your mum and dad will spend as much time with you as they can but it's good to see other people too, especially friends your own age. Perhaps your parents could bring your best friend with them sometimes.

Ask your visitors for their Get Well Soon messages and autographs!

DID YOU KNOW?

If you are well enough, the nurses may be happy for you to go out of the ward for a while with your visitors. You could go for a walk round the hospital or even visit a nearby shop or park. Ask if it's all right before you leave – don't just vanish.

ADULT WARDS

Very occasionally children are treated in adult wards. It's fairly unlikely to happen to you, but if it does, it will probably be because you need specialized nursing care which the children's ward can't provide. If you're not happy about it, say so and ask if you can move to the children's ward as soon as it's possible.

DID YOU KNOW?

If you are on an adult ward, your parents should be able to visit you whenever they wish even if visiting is officially restricted to certain times of day.

Meeting People

While you are in hospital you'll meet an amazing number of different people. If you're in plaster, it's traditional for them to sign your cast. If you're not, ask them to sign the appropriate sections of this book and see how many autographs you can collect by the end of your stay.

TELLING WHO'S WHO

Years ago this was easy. The doctors were the men in white coats while the nurses were the women in blue dresses, crisp white aprons and neat caps. Today it's more complicated. There are women doctors and male nurses. The crisp aprons and caps have virtually disappeared and very few doctors still wear white coats when working with children.

To help you sort out the confusion, all hospital staff wear badges which tell you their name and their job title. To make matters even easier, doctors often have a stethoscope hung round their necks. A tiny teddy bear clipped onto the stethoscope is a clue that the wearer usually treats children (or is extremely addicted to bears).

Modern nurses' uniforms are usually very different from the dressing-up outfits loved by little girls. In some hospitals, nurses wear brightly coloured aprons over their traditional dresses while in others the dresses have been replaced by trousers or skirts with coloured shirts. There's usually some variation in colour or style to show the different types of nurse.

Perhaps you would like to draw some pictures of nurses on this page. You can show the uniform for your ward or design your own.

Here are some of the other people you may meet:

dietician

play worker

occupational therapist

teacher

porter

physiotherapist

cleaner

BE A DETECTIVE

If the nurse in charge of the ward is a woman, she's called a sister. What's the correct name for a male nurse doing the same job? (Here's a clue – he's not a brother.)

MEDICAL STUDENTS

Some hospitals have schools attached to them which teach people to be doctors. While they are learning, they are called medical students. You'll probably meet some if you are in a teaching hospital. Be kind to them because they are probably just as nervous as you are!

As part of their training, the students have to practise examining patients and finding out what's wrong with them. They may ask if they can practise on you. You don't have to agree if you don't want to but it can be an interesting way to fill the time, especially if you're feeling bored. You may even find that you know more about your illness than they do.

A Hospital Wordsearch

How many of these hidden words can you find?

AMBULANCE   STRETCHER   PATIENT
NURSE   DRESSING   MASK
THERMOMETER   PORTER   THEATRE
STETHOSCOPE   DOCTOR   SYRINGE
MEDICINE   PULSE   TROLLEY
OPERATION   BANDAGE   SURGEON
GOWN   BED

```
A X T U L C E E G N I R Y S O U N T I N
Q A M B U L A N C E P D H S C G F H O J
U O E O D P R U G W Y T B E D T K E P R
I Y P R R S G R R E O I R F K Y G R J Q
S S D C O N R S Y I F E E W K R W M P M
Y F L R T P Y E T C O N U N U P L O S I
E G L U C D B R D J I K D S R Y C M S N
L U O D O B X J O C E U P I M X P E J B
L J S J D V E P I Y F W Y U E C M T B T
O G T O B A T D P N K F E N L D J E O H
R M R O A K E P I R U W E U R S L R K E
T O E Y N M P T F W N F K O F D E O L A
L T T L D U E P O C S O H T E T S N O T
M G C I A I O E F Y X W I T J M B Y M R
O N H K G R N A M N E G P U A M P Y S E
G P E J E E U X L P J R M J G T A I R G
O T R I Y T I O P E R A T I O N W S I P
W G N F P R E P G C U F W T L P T S K T
N L R L U O P I N B Y O G N I S S E R D
T R Y G N P A T I E N T I E X W G I L J
```

Answers on page 114

How Medical Words Work

Here are some of the longest medical words I can find. They are all names of drugs. If you can say them quickly three times in a row, your friends will be very impressed and so will I.

tetrahydrocannabinol

(pronounced tet-ra-high-dro-can-ab-in-ol)

phthalylsulphathiazole

(pronounced thal-ill-sul-far-thigh-a-zole)

demethylchlortetracycline

(dee-meth-I'll-claw-tet-ra-sigh-clean)

To save time, ink and writer's cramp, doctors and nurses often use initials instead of writing words in full. Here are some you may spot on your notes or prescriptions.

N.A.D.	– Nothing Abnormal Discovered
B.D.	– Twice a day
Q.D.S.	– Four times a day
T.D.S.	– Three times a day
O.D.	– Once a day

Although many medical words are very long and impressive, it is sometimes possible to work out what they mean. Here are some clues to help you:

-ITIS (pronounced eye-tis) means inflammation so tonsill**itis** means inflamed tonsils and appendic**itis** means an inflamed appendix (If something is inflamed it is swollen and sore.)

-ECTOMY means surgical removal so tonsill**ectomy** means having your tonsils removed and append**ectomy** means having your appendix out.

OLIGO- means too few so **oligo**dontia means too few teeth

DYS- (pronounced dis-) means abnormal, difficult, painful or faulty so **dys**uria means it hurts when you wee and **dys**pepsia means indigestion

A- or **AN-** means absence of, so **a**pyrexia means absence of fever (If someone says you are apyrexial, they mean your temperature is normal.) **an**orexia means absence of appetite and **an**aesthetic means a drug which produces an absence of feeling.

-SCOPE means an instrument for looking at or examining things; so a stetho**scope** is for examining your chest, an oto**scope** is for examining your ear, an endo**scope** is for looking inside your body, and a broncho**scope** is for looking inside your lungs.

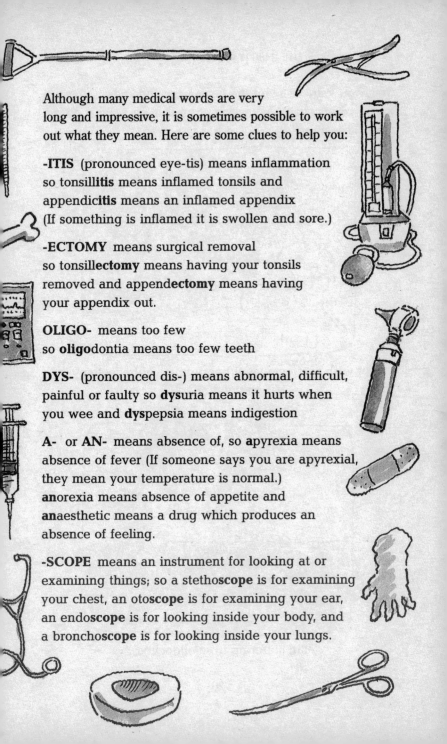

Once you know some of the beginnings and ends of medical words, you can have fun making up pretend ones. What do you think these mean?

'I wish someone would perform a cabbagectomy on my dinner.'

'I'm suffering from oligochocs.'

Doctors and nurses use medical words so much that they often forget that other people don't understand them. If someone uses a word you don't know, ask them to explain it. You can write it down here if you want to remember it.

It's So Embarrassing

Some people love to act or sing and really enjoy speaking in public. Others are shy and don't like to do anything which makes people look at them. Neither group is better than the other. They're just different.

It's the same when it comes to how people feel about their bodies. Some don't mind being seen without their clothes on but many people do, especially if they think they're too fat or too thin or that their skins are too pimply. That's just the way people are.

There's nothing wrong with being shy and it's certainly not babyish. In fact, little children happily toddle around with nothing on. They only start to feel awkward about it as they grow older.

So you're not being silly if you feel shy about letting anyone see the parts of you which are usually covered up. That's just the way you are and lots of people feel the same. The difficulty is that the doctors and nurses may need to look at those bits of you in order to find out exactly what's wrong and make you better. Here's some ideas which may make you feel happier about it.

YOU ARE ENTITLED
TO SOME PRIVACY

Just because the doctor needs to see
you undressed, it doesn't mean
everyone else should as well.
Doctors and nurses are usually
very good about this but if
someone does forget to pull the
curtains round your bed, you're
allowed to remind them.

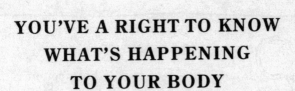

You may feel more confident if your
mum, dad or favourite nurse is with you.
On the other hand, you may prefer that
they're not. Be confident and say exactly what you'd like.

YOU'VE A RIGHT TO KNOW
WHAT'S HAPPENING
TO YOUR BODY

You'll probably feel better about taking off your clothes if you
understand why it's necessary and if you know what's going to
happen next. If no one tells you, ask. If necessary, keep asking
until you get an answer you understand.

YOU'LL GET USED TO IT

Really! You will! Honest! Everyone says so. You'll probably never get to enjoy it but, however embarrassed you feel at first, each time it happens you'll feel a bit more confident.

NO ONE'S GOING TO LAUGH AT YOU

A man lost in a desert would be overjoyed if he saw a drop of water. Put the same man in a rowing boat in the middle of the Atlantic Ocean and he would hardly notice one particular drop, let alone get excited about it.

The doctors and nurses are like the man in the rowing boat. Your bare bottom is just one drop in the vast ocean of bottoms they will see in their lifetimes. They are not going to get excited about it or laugh at it or giggle in the canteen about it saying, 'Guess whose bottom I saw this morning?'!

BE A DETECTIVE

If one nurse sees twenty bare bottoms every day, how many bare bottoms will she see in a) one week?

        b) one year?

        c) forty years?

(If you are feeling really enthusiastic, try multiplying your answers by the number of nurses on your ward.)

BEDPANS AND BOTTLES

If it's totally impossible for you to get out of bed and go to the toilet, you will need to use a bedpan or (if you're a boy and you only want to wee) a bottle. The idea probably doesn't appeal to you very much (it doesn't to most people) but you will get used to it. Anyway, let's face it, if you can't get out of bed, the alternative is much worse.

If you feel embarrassed, say so. The nurses will understand and try to make it easier for you if they can. It might also help to talk about your worries with other children in the same situation. They probably felt exactly like you at first.

You may feel happier being helped by one of the older nurses or a nurse the same sex as yourself. If that's the case, say so or no one will know.

Here are some of the most common worries people have. Perhaps some of yours are the same.

The bedpan looks as if it's made of cardboard. Surely it will leak or go soggy.

No it won't. Modern disposable bedpans and bottles really are waterproof even if they don't look it.

When I wee, it makes so much noise that everyone else in the ward must be able to hear it.

It's nowhere near as loud as you think but, even if they do hear, what does it matter? Everyone has to wee sometime.

If I do a pooh, everyone will smell it.

Hospital wards are big so the smell
vanishes very quickly. If you find this
a real problem, talk to the nurses. It
may be possible to open a window
at a strategic moment or use an air
freshener to give you more
confidence.

*If I do a pooh, who will wipe my
bottom?*

If you can't manage it yourself,
a nurse will do it for you.
Remember yours is just another
drop in the ocean of
bottoms . . .

*Can I wash my
hands
afterwards?*

Yes. Ask your
nurse to
organize this
for you if she
doesn't do it
automatically.

When the nurse takes the bedpan away, everyone will see what I've done.

No, they won't. She'll put a cloth or paper towel over the top.

When I sit on the bedpan, I'm so nervous that I can't go.

Don't worry about it. Just try again later. You'll manage eventually. It's a biological certainty.

FINDING THE RIGHT WORDS

Wee and pooh seem to be universally acceptable words – everyone knows what they mean and everyone's comfortable using them. You may cause raised eyebrows if you use some of the ruder words but it's better to do that than fail to say what you mean.

The medical terms for weeing are 'to pass urine' (sometimes abbreviated to P.U.), 'pass water' and 'urinate'. If a doctor asks 'How are your waterworks?', he is not remotely interested in the well-being of your local water supply company. He just wants to know if you are managing to wee all right.

Other vague terms you may hear used (especially by older people) are 'spending a penny' and 'doing number ones'.

The correct names for pooh are 'stools' or 'faeces' (it rhymes with pieces). Doing a pooh is called 'opening your bowels' or 'passing a motion'. Other terms include 'going with paper' and 'doing number twos'.

I must admit here that I have failed to find out whether doing number ones and number twos at the same time means you've done number threes ...

It's not just going to the toilet which can leave you lost for words. You may also wonder what to call the parts of your body which you don't usually talk about. The safest bet is to use their proper names – penis, testicle, vagina, nipple, etc. Slang words and unusual names can easily be misunderstood. If you're really stuck for the right word, try pointing!

A WORD FOR THE GIRLS

If you've already started your periods and think you might have one while you are in hospital, it's a good idea to take some pads or tampons with you. If you forget them or you're not sure where to put used pads, ask one of the nurses.

If you start unexpectedly (perhaps for the first time), don't be too embarrassed to admit it. All the women nurses and doctors have periods too so they'll know how to help. Remember, having periods is a sign you're growing up – it's not something to be ashamed of.

The Body Quiz

1. You should clean your teeth regularly because:

a) your arm needs the exercise.

b) it keeps your teeth and gums healthy.

c) it provides work for people who make toothpaste.

2. Your blood is red because:

a) You drink plenty of blackcurrant juice.

b) it helps you to see where you have cut yourself.

c) it contains red blood cells which carry oxygen around your body.

3. The semi-circular canals are:

a) circular canals which haven't grown up yet.

b) part of your ear.

c) London's new transport network.

4. The coloured part of your eye is called:

a) your daffodil.

b) your tulip.

c) your iris.

5. Your humerus is:

a) the bone in your upper arm.

b) your sense of humour.

c) the sound you make when you can't remember the words.

33

6. Insulin is:

a) a layer of fat which keeps you warm.

b) a chemical which controls the amount of sugar in your blood.

c) a rude comment.

7. Ligaments are:

a) chewy sweets

b) creams to rub on your face to prevent wrinkles.

c) the tough bands which hold your joints together.

8. The reason your heart beats is:

a) to pump your blood around your body.

b) to give you a sense of rhythm.

c) to let you know where it is.

9. The main purpose of your lungs is:

a) to help you blow up balloons.

b) to provide your body with oxygen.

c) to stop the space inside your chest from going to waste.

10. Sweating is:

a) the way your body cools itself.

b) the remains of a primitive defence mechanism against sabre tooth tigers.

c) your body's overflow system when you drink too much.

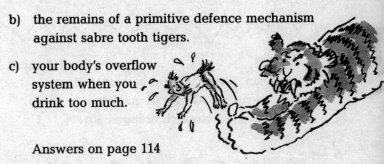

Answers on page 114

Why not try and make up a quiz like this yourself and try it on your visitors or the person in the bed next to you? Your quiz doesn't have to be about the human body – you could write one about your favourite hobby.

Down To Basics

Keep your eyes open and see how many points you can score by spotting this basic equipment. There's some bonus points to be won too. We'll start with an easy one.

CURTAINS   **5 points**

I mean the ones round the beds not the ones at the windows.

BED TABLE   **5 points**

BONUS   **10 points**

If you can design a better bed table. You could include some useful gadgets – how about one to catch dropped jigsaw pieces?

HOSPITAL COT   **55 points**

BE A DETECTIVE

The mattress in a hospital cot is much higher than in an ordinary one. Why?

BED   **5 points**

A hospital bed is different from your one at home. It can be made higher, lower or tilted and it has an adjustable backrest so you can sit up comfortably.

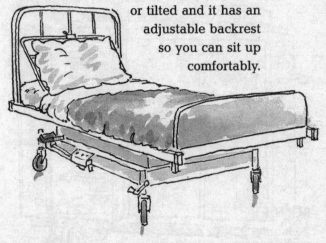

BE A DETECTIVE

Do you wind a handle or press a foot pedal to change the height of your bed? BEWARE – If yours is pedal operated, be careful who you tell. Over enthusiastic use by gadget-mad parents can cause sea-sickness.

37

BEDSIDE LOCKER   5 points

Lockers vary in style – some have
hanging space but others don't. Claim
your points for any type.

FOOD TROLLEY   5 points

This brings all the meals from the
hospital kitchen.

TROLLEY   5 points

Trolleys are used to move people
around the hospital, especially to and
from operations. You may lie on one
instead of a bed if you are having day
surgery or you are in casualty.

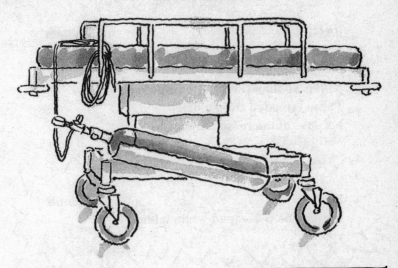

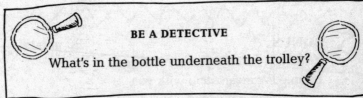

BE A DETECTIVE

What's in the bottle underneath the trolley?

STERILE PACKS   **10 points**

To prevent infection, some dressings
and other equipment are sealed in
paper bags before use and exposed to
a low dose of radiation to kill all the
germs. Don't worry – that doesn't mean
they are radio-active.

BE A DETECTIVE

What colour is the strip on the pack if
it has been sterilized?

PAGER   5 points

Some people who work in more than
one part of the hospital have radio
pagers so they can be contacted easily.
These are often called 'bleeps'
because of the noise they make.

BONUS   5 points

If someone is bleeped while talking to
you.

BONUS   20 points

If someone with a pager manages a
complete conversation with you
without being bleeped.

CONTROL PANEL   5 points

The control panel on the wall by your
bed probably has a light switch and a
button to call the nurse. The handset
lets you operate these controls while
you are in bed. It may also let you listen
to the radio. Perhaps your hospital has
its own radio station.

40

BONUS   **5 points**

If you listen to hospital radio.

BONUS   **5 points**

If your request is played on hospital radio.

HOSPITAL GOWN   **5 points**

Definitely not the latest fashion, but a very practical outfit for the discerning patient about to have an operation and versatile enough to also be worn sometimes for treatments or tests. Designed to be large and baggy so a small range of sizes fit a wide range of people, it has an opening down the back which ties up with tapes.

DID YOU KNOW?

You can usually wear your pants underneath your hospital gown – ask your nurse if you're not sure.

IDENTIFICATION BAND   5 points

Just in case you forget who you are! You
can keep it as a souvenir
when you go home.

THERMOMETER   5 points

STETHOSCOPE   5 points

BONUS   5 points

If you listen to your own chest through
a stethoscope.

AUROSCOPE OR
OTOSCOPE
5 points

This is the gadget doctors use to look
inside your ears.

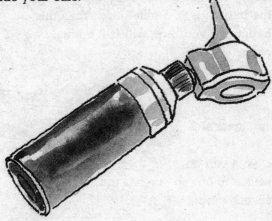

BONUS
1000 points

If you use one to look inside your own
ear.

SPHYGMOMANOMETER
10 points

This mouthful of a name (pronounced
sfig-mo-ma-nom-it-er) belongs to the
gadget which measures your blood
pressure. The doctor or nurse puts an
inflatable cuff around your arm and
pumps air into it until she can no

longer hear the pulse in your arm through her stethoscope. The cuff gets very tight but it doesn't hurt. Then she slowly lets the air out until she hears the pulse again. You'll know when this happens – your arm will feel normal again.

Some modern sphygmomanometers work automatically – you still have a cuff on your arm but no one has to use a stethoscope.

BONUS   **10 points**
If you can say SPHYGMOMANOMETER quickly three times in a row.

BE A DETECTIVE

Blood pressure is always given as two numbers – the pressure when the pulse stops and when it starts again. What are the names of these two readings?

SYRINGE   **5 points**

NEEDLE   **5 points**

You can tell the size of a needle by looking at the colour of its base where it joins the syringe. Orange needles are shorter and finer than blue ones which, in turn, are smaller than green ones.

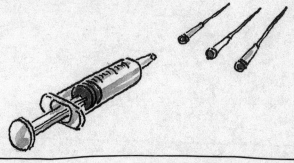

DID YOU KNOW?

Used syringes and needles are dangerous. If you prick yourself with one, you could become very ill. NEVER touch a syringe or needle unless a doctor or nurse tells you to.

Total Score   **points**

Autographs

Crossword

ACROSS

1: Storage cupboards beside the beds. (7)

4: Do your nurses wear this? (7)

7: Definitely not early. (4)

8: Not the beginning. (3)

9: Spiders have lots more than you. (4)

10: Rearrange 'veer' to make this word. (4)

11: Not pretend. (4)

12: It's wet, red and inside you. (5)

14: It hurts if you are _____ by a bee. (5)

16: Babies are _____ when they eat. (5)

19: A group of three together. (4)

20: Way out. (4)

22: Drawings to show how to build a house. (5)

26: You'll need this to use the payphone. (5)

27: Do you clean your teeth _____ day? (5)

28: You'll learn your way around if you go on a _____ of the hospital. (4)

29: People go on one to lose weight. (4)

31: How many times can you have your tonsils out? (4)

32: Long, thin fish. (3)

33: Is your hospital bed made of this metal? (4)

34: Green precious stone. (7)

35: Do this to an orange to get the juice. (7)

CROSSWORD

DOWN

1: A song to send you to sleep. (7)

2: This lets your leg bend. (4)

3: Free from germs. (7)

4: You do this every night before you go to bed. (7)

5: If you _____ out of a tree, you may end up in hospital. (4)

6: If you were shipwrecked, you could send a _____ in a bottle. (7)

13: Frequently. (5)

15: Undo a knot. (5)

16: If you spill your drink, you'll need this to clean up. (3)

17: Large area of salt water. (3)

18: Opposite of 'no'. (3)

21: Even the worst medical student will _____ if he practises. (7)

23: Some deaf people do this to understand what you say. (7)

24: Some are used for sewing and others for injections. (7)

25: Used with one of 24 down to give an injection.

28: A drop of liquid from your eye. (4)

30: This goes slowly when you're bored. (4)

Answers on page 115

Ouch That Hurts

Being ill can hurt. A broken leg is painful and so is an aching head, a sore throat or an inflamed appendix. Sometimes getting better hurts too. Have you ever had a sticking plaster pulled off hairy skin or a graze washed with disinfectant that stings?

51

Pain is felt by the nerve endings in your body which send messages back to your brain – the more nerve endings are affected, the stronger the pain feels. Your skin has many nerve endings but there are fewer deeper in your body. That's why a graze is often more painful than a deeper cut.

ASKING FOR HELP

It is *not* cowardly to ask the nurses for medicine to stop your pain – it's sensible. Why suffer if you don't need to? You don't have to wait until you are in agony before you ask either. There are several different medicines which can help so asking for pain relief doesn't automatically mean you'll have an injection.

Everyone varies in the way they feel pain so the nurses will find it difficult to judge how much something is hurting you unless you tell them. Try to describe the type of pain too. Are you sore, do you ache or is it a sharp pain like a jab from a knife? Is it the same all the time or worse at certain times of day or when you move?

This chart may help you describe how you feel.

HELPING YOURSELF

Pain often feels worse if you are frightened or tense and, of course, you may well feel frightened or tense if you are in pain. One way to break this vicious circle is to take away your fear of the unknown. Ask your doctor or nurse to explain what is hurting, why it's hurting and how long it's likely to last.

If you are having an uncomfortable test done, ask someone to keep you in touch with how it's progressing. It's amazing how much calmer the words 'nearly over' can make you feel.

You may also feel better if you make a deliberate attempt to relax. Breathe slowly and deeply, shut your eyes and imagine you are in your favourite place. You could also try listening to gentle music.

DO SOMETHING ELSE

Have you ever noticed how you hardly feel bangs and bumps when you're in the middle of your favourite sport but a slight ache can seem unbearable when you're lying quietly in bed at night? The same principle is true in hospital. If you keep your mind busy, you won't think about your aches and pains so much so they won't seem as bad. You can:

- Watch interesting programmes on TV

- Read a book with an exciting story

- Play computer games or board games

- Talk or tell jokes

- Do puzzles

- Make a model, knit or sew

- Listen to music, story tapes or the radio

- Persuade someone to read to you

- Write letters to your friends and impress them with all the long words you have learnt

- Write a book and send it to the publishers of this one (address on page ii)

AVOIDING PAIN

If you're going to have a test or treatment which everyone knows will hurt, it's possible to use medicines called anaesthetics (pronounced an-is-thet-iks) to stop the pain before it even starts. There are two types – general anaesthetics and local ones.

A general anaesthetic affects your whole body. It makes you sleep very deeply so you don't feel what's happening.

A local anaesthetic doesn't make you sleep. It only affects the part of you immediately around (local to) the place where the test or treatment will happen. It stops the nerve endings in that area from sending pain messages to your brain. The effect wears off gradually after the treatment is over. You may have already had a local anaesthetic at the dentist if you have had a tooth filled.

EMLA cream is a local anaesthetic which numbs your skin before you have a blood test or other treatment involving a needle. It takes about an hour to work so it needs to be put on well in advance. Once it's taken effect, you can feel the needle moving but it doesn't hurt. It's so effective that it's often called 'magic cream'.

DID YOU KNOW?

EMLA stands for Eutectic Mixture of Local Anaesthetics. The two medicines in it are mixed together in such a way that they are more effective together than they would be separately.

DRESSING CHANGES

There are two views on taking off sticking plasters. There's the 'if it's going to hurt you might as well pull it off quickly and get it over with' club and the 'slower the better' one. Ask the nurse to do it whichever way you prefer. You may find it helps to take the plaster off yourself. It seems to hurt less – perhaps that's because you are in control. Sometimes moistening the edges of the plaster with water helps too.

WHEN YOU'RE FED UP

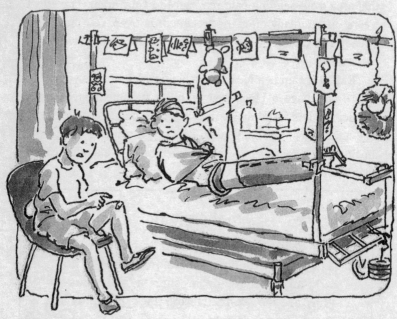

Being in hospital doesn't always feel good. There may be times when you feel fed up with being ill, angry about what's happening to you or just plain homesick. Remember there's nothing wrong with crying. It's not babyish and might make you feel better. You could also

- talk to someone about how you feel – anyone will do as long as you feel comfortable with them;

- write down how you feel. Afterwards you can tear it up and throw it away if you like – there's no need to show it to anyone unless you want to;

- use up some of your anger by hitting a pillow or soft toy or banging some playdough (ask the play worker for some).

Limericks

There was a young doctor from Fife
Who ate garlic each day of his life.
The nurses – they moaned,
The patients all groaned,
But the worst complaints came from his wife.

A nurse called Petunia Gorse
Came to work one day riding a horse.
She put it to bed,
Rubbed cream on its head.
It was very soon better, of course.

Limericks are fun to write as well as fun to read. Can you make some up yourself? Here are some first lines to get you started.

A very old patient called Bill

A doctor who travelled by car

There once was a sister called Pat

Testing, Testing

If you have cut your finger, it's easy for the doctors to see what is wrong. But they can't always find out what's happening inside you just by looking. That's why they use special tests and investigations to help them.

X-RAYS

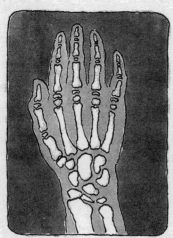

X-rays can go through the soft parts of your body quite easily but they can't go through your bones. An X-ray picture of your hand looks like this. The soft parts of your hand look grey or black because X-rays have gone through them and darkened the film. Your bones look white because no X-rays have gone through them.

Before you have an X-ray, you will have to remove any jewellery or metal fastenings which would show up on the picture. You may also have to take off some of your clothes and put on a hospital gown.

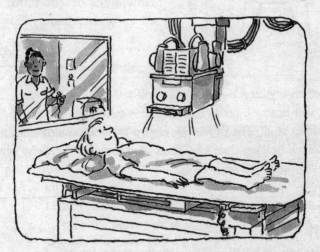

Some X-rays are taken with you lying down but you may have to stand or sit depending on which part of you is being photographed. There are no X-rays coming out of the machine while the radiographer adjusts it – she uses a beam of ordinary light to show her where they will go.

She only wants the X-rays to go through you so she and anyone else in the room will either go behind a screen while the picture is taken or wear a lead apron (X-rays can't go through lead).

BE A DETECTIVE

How much do you think a lead apron weighs?

When everything is ready, she will tell you to stay very still. You will hear a buzz as the picture is taken but you won't feel anything at all. The film is developed by a processing machine. It's much quicker than when you send away your holiday snaps – it only takes 90 seconds.

BE A DETECTIVE

The film is in a flat metal box called a cassette – see if you can spot where she puts it. It must be the other side of you from the source of the X-rays.

DID YOU KNOW?

Inside the cassette, the film goes between two flat surfaces which glow when X-rays hit them – the more X-rays there are, the brighter they glow. The surfaces are called intensifying screens because the light they produce makes the picture clearer (more intense).

CT SCANS

CT is short for computed tomography. That means it uses a computer to turn a series of X-ray pictures taken from different angles into one picture which looks like a slice through your

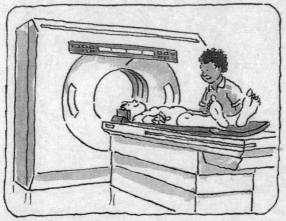

body. It's good at looking at your brain and other parts of you which don't show up well on ordinary X-ray pictures.

When you have a scan, you lie on a bed which slides forward so the part of you being examined is inside the ring of the machine. The top of the ring is fairly close to you but don't worry – it won't move any nearer. If you don't like looking at it, it may help to close your eyes.

You won't feel the scan being done but you will hear a whirring sound for a few seconds as each set of pictures is taken. After each set, the bed will move forward slightly to put you in the right position for the next one. The bed moves very gently – can you feel it?

MRI SCAN

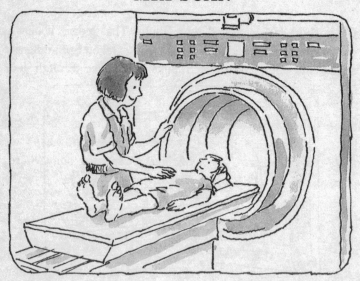

An MRI scanner also uses a computer to produce pictures of slices through your body but it doesn't use X-rays. Instead it uses radio waves and a magnet which is so strong that if you went in the scanner with a metal pen in your pocket it would be sucked out.

An MRI scanner looks very similar to a CT one but the ring is much longer. It's more like a tunnel and your whole body goes inside at once. The scanner is quite noisy while it is working but you won't feel anything.

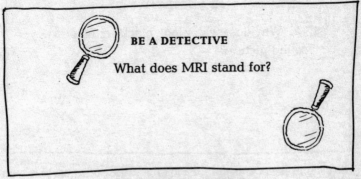

BE A DETECTIVE

What does MRI stand for?

STAYING STILL

It's very important to lie still during a CT or MRI scan. To make this easier, you may be given some medicine beforehand to make you feel sleepy. Try imagining you're lying somewhere pleasant like a warm beach or your own bed.

ULTRASOUND

Ultrasound scanning works in a similar way to the sonar location used by submarines and bats. The scanner sends very high frequency sound (too high for you to hear) into your body and listens to the way the sound bounces back (or echoes). A computer turns the echoes into a picture of the inside of you. Strong echoes from air or bone show as white while the softer echoes from other parts of you show as various shades of grey.

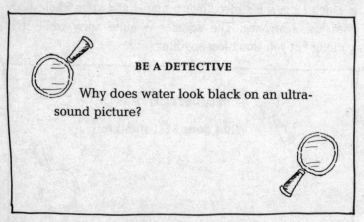

BE A DETECTIVE

Why does water look black on an ultrasound picture?

Ultrasound is very useful for looking at the softer parts of you which don't show up well on an X-ray. It makes a moving picture, so it can show how your heart is beating and how fast your blood is moving. Pregnant mums often have scans to see how the baby is growing. Ask your mum if she saw an ultrasound picture of you before you were born.

When you have an ultrasound scan, you lie on a bed and the radiographer puts some cold, slimy jelly on the area she's going to examine. Then she slides an object which looks like a microphone across your skin – it sends out the sound and picks up the echoes. (It's called a *transducer* because it changes the sound of the echoes into electrical signals which the computer uses to make the pictures.) The jelly is there to make sure there is no air between the transducer and your skin.

If you ask, she may be able to move the screen so that you can see it too. The picture is rather fuzzy so you'll probably need help to understand what you are seeing (I always do).

You won't feel the sound at all, just the transducer moving across your skin. If you are already sore, you may feel uncomfortable if the radiographer has to press firmly but it won't last for very long.

BLOOD TESTS

Your blood can tell the doctors a great deal about how well your body is working. Sometimes they just need a single drop of blood from a finger prick. Usually they need more than that so they'll take some from your arm. That's not because there's anything special about the blood in your arm – it's the same as everywhere else in your body. It's just that it's quite easy to take it from the large veins on the inside of your elbow.

BE A DETECTIVE

Look at the inside of your elbow. Can you see your veins? They look like blue lines. Can you see some on the backs of your hands too?

Before they take the blood, they'll tie a strap round your upper arm or squeeze it with their hands. This makes the veins become fatter and easier to see.

Most people don't like having blood tests, which isn't surprising. However, they're not usually as bad as you've imagined, especially if you've had EMLA (magic cream) on your arm (see page 89). If you haven't, they can use a special spray instead which feels incredibly cold and makes your skin go numb. Remember that even if it does hurt a little, it will soon be over.

If you're worried, try looking the other way and thinking about something completely different – talking or telling jokes helps (provided you keep off the subject of vampires).

BE A DETECTIVE

They nearly always use a green coded needle for a blood test. Can you find out why?

Your blood is collected in a syringe and then put in small tubes ready to be sent to the lab for testing. It may look like a lot of blood but it's not really. Even 20 mls (which looks like a vast amount in a syringe) is only two tablespoonsful and your body will soon make some more. Anyway you'll have plenty left – the exact amount depends on how big you are. An average-sized adult has about 5 litres.

BE A DETECTIVE

I have only written about a few of the tests you may have. If you have a different one, try to find out:

What was the test called?

What was it for?

How was it done?

Did you like it?

The Hospital Highway Code

Keep a look out for these signs and notices as you move around the hospital. Each one earns you 10 points. You can count any sign which has the same meaning, even if it doesn't look exactly the same as the one here.

Temperature Chart

Nil by Mouth   This patient mustn't eat or drink anything.

Sips Only   This patient is just starting to drink again.

Bed Rest   No, this one's not for tired furniture. It's the patient who must stay in bed and rest.

Isolation   If you see this notice outside a room, the person inside is being kept away from other patients. It may either be to protect him from other people's germs or to protect everyone else from his.

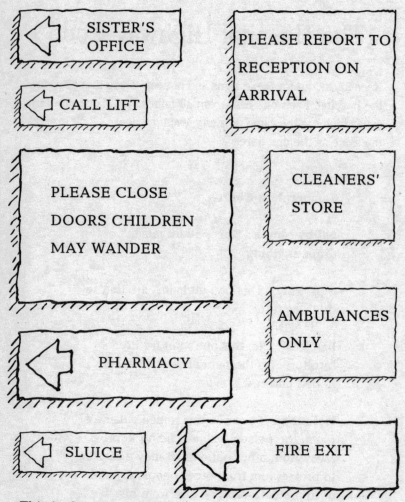

⟵ SISTER'S OFFICE

⟵ CALL LIFT

PLEASE REPORT TO RECEPTION ON ARRIVAL

PLEASE CLOSE DOORS CHILDREN MAY WANDER

CLEANERS' STORE

⟵ PHARMACY

AMBULANCES ONLY

⟵ SLUICE

⟵ FIRE EXIT

This is the room for the messy jobs like emptying the bedpans.

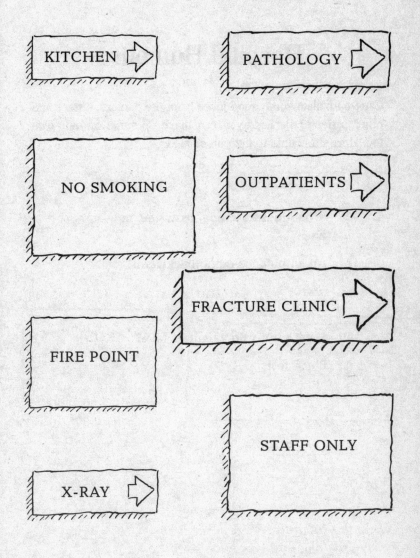

TOTAL SCORE

Hospital Humour

Can you collect some good jokes from the doctors, nurses and other patients? Perhaps you can make up some of your own too. Here's a couple to get you started.

Q: **What goes naw, nee, naw, nee, naw, nee . . .?**

A: An ambulance going backwards.

Q: **What exams do vampires take?**

A: Blood tests.

GIGGLES
& CHUCKLES

TO BE TAKEN
GAILY

Taking The Medicine

All medicines are drugs so that's what they are usually called in hospital. It's perfectly all right to take drugs when you are told to by a doctor or nurse. The warnings you get at school are about *abusing* drugs – that means taking them without being told to by a doctor or without following the instructions on the packet. That is very dangerous and can make you ill or even kill you.

At home, you usually take medicine by swallowing tablets or a liquid, rubbing cream on your skin or putting drops in your eyes, nose or ears. In hospital, there are other methods you can use too.

INJECTIONS

You won't be given an injection unless it's absolutely necessary. There are some drugs which you can't swallow because they would be damaged or destroyed by the juices which digest your food. There are also times when you need an injection because you can't drink or you need the medicine to work very quickly.

Injections?
I can't stand 'em!

DID YOU KNOW?

Once the point has gone through your skin, you'll hardly notice the rest of the needle follow it. It's quite likely that you won't feel the medicine go into you either but it may feel cold if it's just come out of the fridge or it may sting a little.

Some people say an injection feels like a scratch. Others think it is like a prick from a pin. Either way, there is no disguising the fact that injections hurt. But the good thing is they don't hurt for long. It helps if you can relax. Try talking or thinking about something completely different. You could count the tiles on the wall (if there are any), tell the nurse about your favourite TV programme or ask her for a contribution to the jokes page.

BE A DETECTIVE

If you have an injection:
What colour code is the needle?

Is the injection:
to kill the germs making you ill?
to make you sleepy?
to take away your pain?
to do something else?

INTRAVENOUS TREATMENT

Intravenous treatment (IV for short) means putting a liquid directly into one of your veins – they carry blood around your body and look like thin blue lines under your skin. The liquid (which might be medicine, blood or anything else you need) goes straight into your blood and is carried quickly around your body.

If you need intravenous treatment, the doctor will put a very thin plastic tube called a cannula (or line) into a vein in your arm or the back of your hand. You'll probably have some EMLA (magic cream) put on before she starts (see page 55).

The tube has a needle down the centre of it which the doctor pushes into your vein. The tube slides in with the needle and, once it is in place, the doctor takes the needle out. Only the plastic tube stays in your arm.

The cannula is held in place with sticky tape and can safely stay there for several days. You'll probably also have a bandage and splint put on to stop you bending that part of your arm.

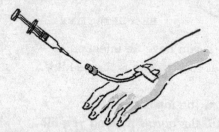

Sometimes you can't feel the tube is there but your arm may be sore or ache. If you are worried about it or it hurts a lot, tell the nurses.

Your medicine can be injected through the end of the tube without having to prick you with any more needles.

Alternatively the liquid you need can be put in a bag and allowed to drip slowly into your vein. The speed at which the fluid goes in may be controlled by an electric pump. The pump will bleep loudly from time to time. Don't worry – it's not an emergency. It's just reminding the nurses that it needs to be checked.

You don't have to stay in bed just because you are on a drip. Provided you are well enough, you can go to the playroom or the toilet in the normal way – the drip stand has wheels so you can take it with you.

It's quite likely that you won't feel the liquid going in. If it stings or hurts in any other way, tell the nurses. They may be able to put the medicine in more slowly or do something else to make you feel more comfortable.

BE A DETECTIVE

If you are having IV treatment:
Where is your cannula?
What liquid are you being given through it?

INHALERS AND NEBULIZERS

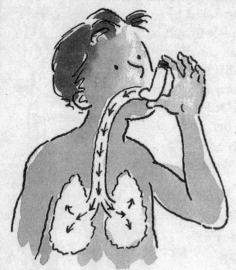

If you have a cough or find it difficult to breathe, you can take some medicine that goes straight into your lungs: an inhaler lets you breathe in the drug as a powder.

You can also breathe in the drug using a nebulizer which turns liquids into a fine mist.

DID YOU KNOW?

Although the mist looks like steam, it's not. The nebulizer makes the mist by passing compressed gas through the liquid which breaks up into thousands of tiny droplets. It works in a similar way to a household aerosol can but it only uses ordinary air or oxygen so it's totally ozone friendly.

SUPPOSITORIES

A suppository is made of a wax-like substance with the drug mixed into it. It's small and cone-shaped so that it can be pushed gently inside your bottom (or rectum, as the doctors call it).

The idea probably doesn't appeal to you very much but it's nowhere near as bad as you might imagine. It's a strange sensation but doesn't really hurt, especially if you relax and think of something else. Telling jokes can keep your mind off what's happening too. Perhaps the nurse can provide some new ones for your collection.

Having a suppository is sometimes an alternative way to take a medicine which would otherwise have to be injected. Although you may think it sounds rather undignified, many people prefer it to having another jab from a needle.

A Medical Trivia Quiz

(When you have tried this yourself, why not see how
well your nurse can do?)

1. Who was the nurse with the lamp in the Crimean
   War?

2. Which medicine was originally obtained from
   crushed willow bark?

3. Which fictional doctor can travel through space
   and time?

4. What did Willhelm Konrad Rontgen discover in
   1895?

5. Sir Alexander Fleming discovered the first
   antibiotic in 1928. What is it called?

6. Which British king had to postpone his coronation so that he could have an urgent operation?

7. Where is your hallux?

8. Which is the longest bone in your body?

9. In which country was the first human heart transplant performed?

10. Years ago many sailors on long voyages suffered from scurvy because something was missing from their diet. Which foods did they need to keep them well?

Answers on page 116

Operations

Before you have an operation, one of the doctors will explain what is going to happen. This is a good chance to ask questions about anything you don't understand. He will also ask your mum or dad to sign a form giving their permission for the doctors to operate on you.

To make sure you don't feel anything during the operation, you'll be given some medicine (an anaesthetic) to make you sleep very deeply. It's not the same as normal sleep so you won't wake up if you are moved around or hear a loud noise.

A doctor called an anaesthetist will give you the medicine and look after you while the operation is happening. He will make sure you stay asleep until it's all over and make sure you wake up afterwards. He'll come to see you on the ward before the operation – try to get his (or her) autograph for your collection.

DID YOU KNOW?

Doctors who perform operations are called surgeons. It's traditional in Britain to call them Mr, Mrs or Miss instead of Doctor. This comes from centuries ago when operations were carried out by barbers rather than proper doctors. That's not true any more so there's no point in asking your surgeon to cut your hair!

Some people have amazing dreams when they have an anaesthetic but others don't dream at all (or they don't remember anyway). If I could choose, I would dream about galloping fast on a white horse with its mane and tail streaming in the wind. Can you design your perfect dream? You can write about it here or draw a picture.

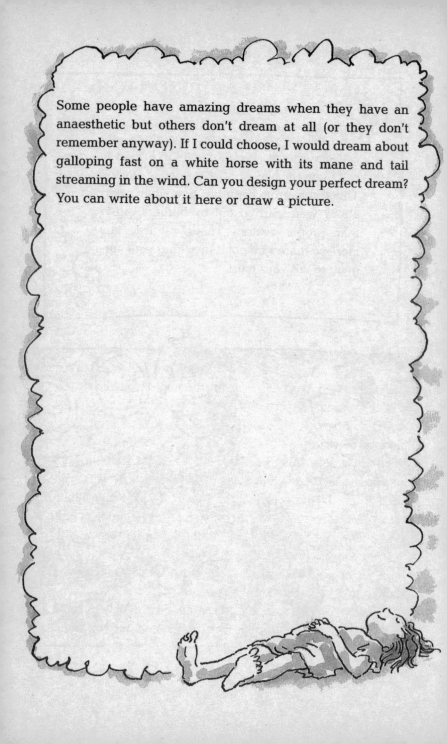

BEFORE YOUR OPERATION

Your operation will happen in a room called a theatre which is kept very clean and free from germs. The people who work there wear special clothes and shoes instead of their outdoor ones. Don't expect them to do a song and dance routine – it's not that sort of theatre.

It's important not to eat or drink anything for a few hours before your operation to make sure you're not sick while you're asleep. You'll have a notice on your bed saying 'NIL BY MOUTH' to remind everyone.

Before you go to theatre, you'll put on a hospital gown. It's often all right to keep your pants on underneath – ask your nurse if you're not sure. You'll probably have some EMLA or magic cream on your hand and you may also have some medicine called a pre-med which will make you feel relaxed and sleepy. Pre-med is short for pre-medication – a medicine you take before something happens.

The nurses will remake your bed so you are lying on a piece of canvas with a slot down each side. When the porters bring the trolley to fetch you, they can slide a pole into the hem on each side of the canvas to make a stretcher with you already on it. Don't get too excited though. If you're wide awake when they bring the trolley to fetch you, they'll probably ask you to climb on by yourself. If it's not far to the theatre, you may even be asked to walk!

Your mum or dad can go to theatre with you and may be allowed to stay until you are asleep.

Whichever way you go to theatre, you'll definitely come back to the ward on a trolley. You'll be asleep but you could

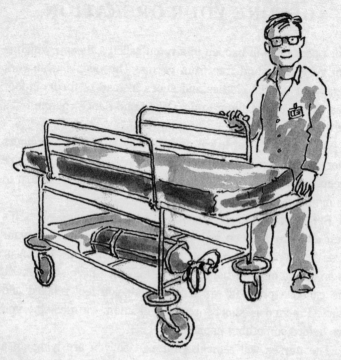

arrange for someone else to collect the porters' autographs for you.

HAVING AN ANAESTHETIC

If your mum goes into the anaesthetic room with you, she may have to wear an overall over her clothes, a cap and plastic overshoes. It's a very unglamorous outfit and nothing like she'd choose for an evening at the theatre. She'll probably feel like a right lemon and so will your dad if he keeps you company instead.

While you are asleep, the anaesthetist will use some elec-tronic equipment to keep a constant check on how your body is working. That's just routine – it's not a sign that the doctors are worried about you. You'll have sticky pads on your chest to measure your heart beat plus a clip on one finger to measure your pulse and how much oxygen there is in your blood. If you can see the monitor working before you go to sleep, see if you can slow down your pulse rate by relaxing and breathing more slowly.

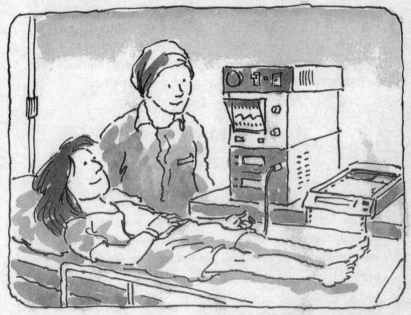

If you haven't already got one, the anaesthetist will put an IV cannula in your hand (see page 80). Then he'll squirt the anaesthetic into it – you'll feel the medicine go up your arm. If he asks you to count to ten, you'll be asleep before you finish – everyone always is.

AFTER THE OPERATION

When the operation is over, you'll stay in the recovery room close to theatre until you have woken up a little but you probably won't remember this afterwards. Don't worry if you have an oxygen mask on your face when you wake up – that's normal and doesn't mean anything is wrong.

When you are just awake but still very sleepy, you'll go back to the ward. The nurses may have moved your bed nearer their desk so they can see you easily without having to walk too far. If you've had a very complicated operation, you may spend some time afterwards on a different ward where there are extra nurses and equipment to look after you. You'll go back to your own ward as soon as you are feeling better.

HOW WILL YOU FEEL AFTERWARDS?

How you feel will depend on what has happened to you. You're almost certain to be sleepy and you may feel sore and uncomfortable. If you're in pain, ask the nurses if you can have some medicine to help you feel better, (see Ouch that Hurts, page 51).

STITCHES AND CLIPS

Not all operations involve cutting your skin. For instance, the doctors can reach your tonsils through your mouth and they can use a flexible tube called an endoscope to see right down your throat and into your stomach. If they do have to cut you, they will use stitches or small metal clips to join the edges of the wound together afterwards.

The stitches or clips are removed once your skin has healed. They come out very easily and often don't hurt at all. Some stitches are made of material which dissolves so they don't need to be taken out.

BE A DETECTIVE

If you're going to have an operation, see how much you can find out before it happens.

Why are you having this operation?

Will you have a pre-med?

How long will the operation take?

How will they reach the part of you they are operating on?

Will you be back in the same place when you wake up? If not, where will you be?

Will you have any stitches or clips? If so, where will they be?

Will you have any tubes or wires attached to you when you wake up?

Word Games

ANAGRAMS

When you rearrange the letters of a word or phrase so that they say something else, you've made an anagram. Can you work out the words from which I made these? I've done the first one already to help you.

> TAIL SHOP   answer – HOSPITAL

1: COD ROT

2: A PINE ROOT

3: BAD PEN

4: CUT RAIN

5: TELL ROY

6: DICE MINE

Why not make up some anagrams yourself to test your friends? Perhaps you can make some funny ones out of people's names.

Answers on page 116

HIDDEN WORDS

How many words can you make out of the letters in

OPERATION

If you score:	
less than 20	have another look
20–29	well done
30–39	good
40–49	very good
50–59	excellent
60–69	genius
70 or over	super genius

Answers on page 116

If you found that easy, try doing the same with

SPHYGMOMANOMETER

THE NAME GAME

If you like playing with words, try making the names of your drugs into characters from a fantasy story.

For instance, there's the amazingly chatty PARROT SAYS-IT-ALL (from PARACETAMOL) and VENT O'LYNN, the daring Irish explorer (from VENTOLIN).

If you are feeling really imaginative, you can write a story for your characters or draw them.

Getting Plastered

Sometimes it's necessary to keep part of your body completely still while it gets better. One reason for this is when you break a bone – the broken pieces have to be kept in exactly the right place so that the bone heals straight.

CASTS

One way to keep part of you still is to surround it with a rigid layer called a cast which is made of resin or plaster of Paris. Resin casts are lighter than plaster ones but much more difficult for your friends to write their names on. Your doctor will decide which type you have.

BE A DETECTIVE

The Cast List

How many of these casts can you spot on other patients?

A lower arm cast   An over elbow cast

A lower leg cast   A full leg cast

A frog (or broomstick) cast

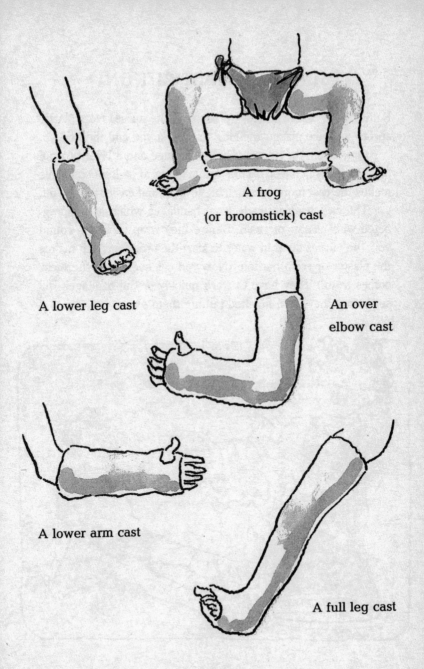

A frog

(or broomstick) cast

A lower leg cast

An over
elbow cast

A lower arm cast

A full leg cast

99

HAVING A CAST PUT ON

Putting on a cast is a messy process so the nurses wear plastic aprons and use plastic sheeting to protect you and the bed.

First of all, they put a tubular bandage and a layer of wool padding on whichever part of you is going to be kept still. This makes the cast more comfortable to wear and easier to take off.

The cast itself is made from bandages which are impregnated with plaster or resin. Before they wrap each one round you, the nurses dip it in water to start the process which makes the plaster or resin harden. (Now you can see where the mess comes from!) They have to work quickly or the bandages will set before they have finished putting them on.

The nurses keep bandaging until the cast feels firm – it takes several layers. On a plaster cast, they rub their wet hands over the top layer to smooth the plaster which has oozed out of the bandages. That's why you can't see the bandages when you look at a finished plaster cast. You can see them easily on a resin cast and you can feel their texture if you run your fingers across its surface.

The cast feels warm as it hardens – it's quite a pleasant feeling. A resin cast sets in 20 minutes and is hard in an hour. A plaster cast also sets quickly but it takes about two days to dry completely.

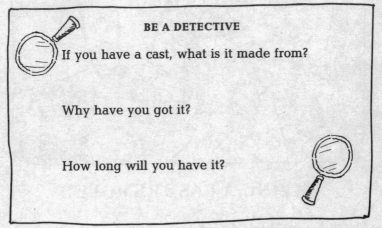

BE A DETECTIVE

If you have a cast, what is it made from?

Why have you got it?

How long will you have it?

LIVING WITH A CAST

Even a lightweight resin cast is surprisingly heavy so it will take you a while to get used to it. Sometimes you may feel itchy inside it but it is important *not* to try scratching by pushing pencils or anything else inside. Ask the nurses what you can do instead.

Casts mustn't get wet so it'll probably be impossible to have a bath. You'll be able to keep clean by washing the unplastered parts of you with a flannel and you can use perfume or deodorant if you are worried you might smell.

HAVING A CAST REMOVED

Sometimes one cast is enough but you may need to have yours changed several times before you are better. This is particularly likely with a long course of treatment as you'll grow out of your cast in the same way as you grow out of your shoes.

The only way to take off a cast is to cut it with an electric plaster saw or special shears. The electric saw looks like a miniature circular saw but, although it looks scary and makes a great deal of noise, it is completely harmless.

The jagged blade doesn't whizz round at lightning speed. In fact, it doesn't turn round at all. Instead it vibrates from side to side to cut through your cast. The padding inside will stop it touching your skin but it wouldn't matter if it did as it's not powerful enough to cut you.

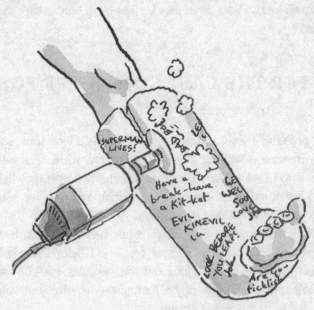

Once the person removing your cast has cut it into two or more pieces, he'll push them apart with a gadget called a spreader. Then he'll cut through the bandage with some long-handled scissors, lift off the pieces of cast and the job's finished. The whole process only takes a few minutes.

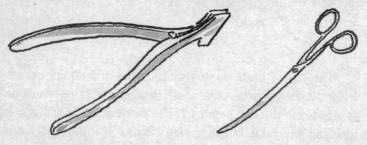

If you want to keep your cast as a souvenir, say so or it will be thrown away. (Your mum may be less keen on this idea than you are.)

AFTER THE CAST COMES OFF FOR GOOD

You'll probably have had the cast on for quite a long time, so it will feel strange without it. The part of you which has been inside it will look different – paler and thinner with dry, flaky skin – but it will soon get back to normal. You can use some moisturiser on your skin if you wish.

Don't be surprised if it takes a while before you can move that part of your body as well as you could before. It will be very stiff after being still so long and your muscles won't be used to doing any work. The physiotherapist may give you some exercises to help you get strong again.

TRACTION

If you break the bone in your thigh, you will probably be treated with traction instead of a cast. That's because the muscles in your thigh tend to pull the broken ends of bone past each other like this.

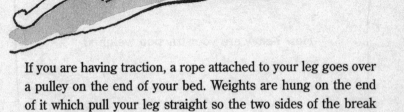

If you are having traction, a rope attached to your leg goes over a pulley on the end of your bed. Weights are hung on the end of it which pull your leg straight so the two sides of the break line up and heal well.

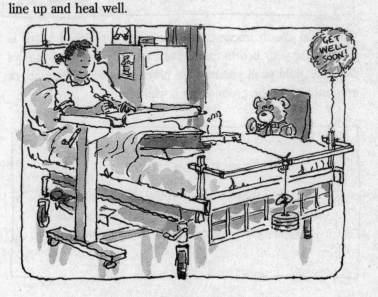

Not everyone having traction has broken their leg. It can be helpful for some other leg and hip problems too.

BE A DETECTIVE

If you are having traction:

Why are you having it?

How heavy are your traction weights?

While you are in traction, you can't get out of bed but it is possible for your bed to move. Perhaps your parents or one of the staff could push you into the playroom, the schoolroom or even outside in the grounds for a while.

BE A GOOD FRIEND

If you are up and about, be careful not to knock other children's traction weights. It's very uncomfortable for them if you do.

PINNED BONES

You may see someone with pins coming out of their arm or leg which are attached to a metal bar. This is another way to hold pieces of broken bone together while they heal but it is only used when the more ordinary methods won't work. It looks extremely painful but it's not. People who have had them say the pins don't hurt unless they are knocked.

How Patient A Patient Are You?

Find out by deciding how you would react to these situations.

1: You've arrived on the ward just in time for dinner and it's fish. You hate fish – it always makes you feel sick. Do you:

    a) Pretend you are not hungry?

    b) Explain your problem and ask if there is anything else you could have instead?

    c) Burst into tears and hide under the bed?

2: The doctor comes to explain your new treatment. Do you:

    a) Ignore him and let your mum do all the talking?

    b) Listen carefully and ask questions about anything you don't understand?

    c) Burst into tears and hide under the bed?

3: After the doctor has gone, you think about a question you forgot to ask. Do you:

    a) Feel cross with yourself but do nothing?

    b) Write down your question so you remember to ask it next time you have the chance?

    c) Burst into tears, sit under the bed and sulk?

4: You are feeling very sore and uncomfortable after your operation. Do you:

    a) Grit your teeth and put up with it because you think pain relief is only for people who are in agony?

    b) Tell the nurse so you can have some medicine to help you feel better?

    c) Burst into tears but refuse to tell anyone what's wrong?

5: You agree to help a medical student but she starts to examine your chest and tummy without pulling the curtains round your bed. Do you:

    a)   Hope no one's looking?

    b)   Ask her to stop what she's doing and pull the curtains?

    c)   Dive under the bed with your box of tissues?

6: A lady has come to take a sample of your blood for testing. You would like your dad to be with you while it's done but he has just gone to the toilet. Do you:

    a)   Manage as best you can without him?

    b)   Ask if she can wait until he comes back?

    c)   Hide under the bed and howl?

Answers on page 117

Useful Addresses

If you need more information or advice about being in hospital, ask the staff on your ward or contact:

ACTION FOR SICK CHILDREN
Argyle House, 29–31 Euston Road,
London NW1 2SD
Tel: 071–833–2041

(Action for Sick Children used to be called NAWCH – the National Association for the Welfare of Children in Hospital)

Action for Sick Children produce a comic for 4–7 year olds and a leaflet for 12 and up. Both cost £1.00.

If you need more information or advice about your illness or disability, phone or write to:

CONTACT A FAMILY
16 Strutton Ground
London SW1P
Tel: 071–222–3969

Be A Detective – Answers

Page 15

A male nurse in charge of a ward is called a charge nurse.

Page 24

If she works every day,

The nurse sees 140 bare bottoms in one week
7300 in one year (365 days)
292000 in forty years

Page 37

The mattress is high so the nurses do not have to bend too much when caring for the baby.

Page 39

The bottle under the trolley contains oxygen.

Page 39

The coloured strip on a sterile pack turns brown when it has been sterilized.

Page 44

When measuring blood pressure:
The reading when the pulse stops is called the SYSTOLIC pressure. The reading when the pulse restarts is called the DIASTOLIC pressure.

Page 64

An adult-size lead apron weighs about 8.5kg.

Page 67
MRI stands for magnetic resonance imaging.

Page 68
Water looks black on an ultrasound picture because there is no echo from it. The sound goes straight through the water without being bounced back (reflected) at all.

Page 71
Green needles are used for bood tests because they are wide enough for the blood to flow through quite easily without damaging the blood cells.

A Hospital Wordsearch – Solution

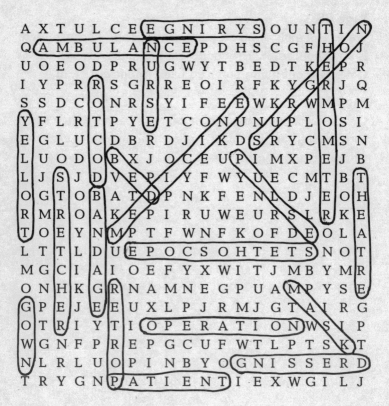

```
A X T U L C E E G N I R Y S O U N T I N
Q A M B U L A N C E P D H S C G F H O J
U O E O D P R U G W Y T B E D T K E P R
I Y P R R S G R R E O I R F K Y G R J Q
S S D C O N R S Y I F E E W K R W M P M
Y F L R T P Y E T C O N U N U P L O S I
E G L U C D B R D J I K D S R Y C M S N
L U O D O B X J O C E U P I M X P E J B
L J S J D V E P I Y F W Y U E C M T B T
O G T O B A T D P N K F E N L D J E O H
R M R O A K E P I R U W E U R S L R K E
T O E Y N M P T F W N F K O F D E O L A
L T T L D U E P O C S O H T E T S N O T
M G C I A I O E F Y X W I T J M B Y M R
O N H K G R N A M N E G P U A M P Y S E
G P E J E E U X L P J R M J G T A I R G
O T R I Y T I O P E R A T I O N W S I P
W G N F P R E P G C U F W T L P T S K T
N L R L U O P I N B Y O G N I S S E R D
T R Y G N P A T I E N T I E X W G I L J
```

The Body Quiz – Answers

1:	b	5:	a	9:	b
2:	c	6:	b	10:	a
3:	b	7:	c		
4:	c	8:	a		

Crossword Solution

ACROSS

1:	lockers		20:	exit
4:	uniform		22:	plans
7:	late		26:	money
8:	end		27:	every
9:	legs		28:	tour
10:	ever		29:	diet
11:	real		31:	once
12:	blood		32:	eel
14:	stung		33:	iron
16:	messy		34:	emerald
19:	trio		35:	squeeze

DOWN

1:	lullaby		17:	sea
2:	knee		18:	yes
3:	sterile		21:	improve
4:	undress		23:	lipread
5:	fall		24:	needles
6:	message		25:	syringe
13:	often		28:	tear
15:	untie		30:	time
16:	mop			

Answers To The Medical Trivia Quiz

1: Florence Nightingale
2: Aspirin
3: Dr Who
4: X-rays
5: Penicillin
6: Edward VII
7: On your foot – it's your big toe
8: Your thigh bone or femur
9: South Africa
10: Fresh fruit and vegetables which contain vitamin C

Wordgames – Answers

ANAGRAMS

1. doctor
2. operation
3. bedpan
4. curtain
5. trolley
6. medicine

HIDDEN WORDS

(These are the ones I've found but
you may find others too.)

a, I, an, at, in, it, no, or, to, ant, ape, are, art, ear, era, ion, ire, nap, net, nip, nit, nor, not, pan, par, pat, pea, pen, pet, pin, pit, pot, ran, rap, rat, rip, rot, tan, tap, tar, tea, ten, tin, tip, ton, toe, tie, too, top, inert, into, iron, nape, near, note, onto, open, opera, pain, pair, pare, pate, pear, pert, pine, poor, pore, rain, rate, ratio, root, rope, rota, rote, tare, tarn, tear, tine, tire, tone, tape, tope, tore, trap, trip, inapt, inept, inter, prone, train, tripe, troop, potion, ration.

How Patient A Patient Are You?

Check Your Score

If your answers are:

Mainly a's **VERY PATIENT**
You don't have to put up with everything quite so much. Why not take a more active interest in what's going on and let people know how you feel?

Mainly b's **PERFECTLY PATIENT**
Good for you. You're taking control of your life instead of letting it just happen.

Mainly c's **IMPATIENT**
There's nothing wrong with crying but getting upset so easily *all* the time could cost you a fortune in tissues. The hospital staff want to help you. Why not make their job easier by talking to them?